William and the Tick Invasion

By Eric Canfield & Lauren Lovejoy
Illustrated by Ari S. Martin

Printed in the United States of America

ISBN-10: 1729635865
ISBN-13: 978-1729635865

The text of this book is set in 16 pt Janda Safe and Sound Font
The illustrations in this book were created digitally

We would like to dedicate this book to the wonderful Sharma, Liz, William and Anthony. Thank you for sharing your family and light with us, and inspiring us to continue to give back to a community with love.
Your way of caring for others is truly inspiring.

All proceeds from this book go to funding for Lyme research.

LYME WARRIOR

William climbed excitedly out of his family's tree house. He had just left home high up in the tree, his big sister Meg waving good-bye. The last of the snow had melted, spring had sprung, and he was excited to play with his friends again.

As he made his way through the woods he couldn't find any of his friends and he started to worry. He stopped to see the rabbits, but they never came to the door.

Neither would the squirrels or the chipmunks.

Suddenly, he heard the stamping of hooves and he became surrounded by deer. At first he was excited, thinking some of his friends had come to play. As the deer came closer however, he saw that they all looked tired and sad. On top of each deer's head, William could see a tick riding, steering the deer by pulling its ears.

Once they had circled William and the dust began to settle, a small voice called out from one of the deer: "What are you doing down here little boy?"

William squinted at the top of the deer's head. A tiny nymph tick clung tightly to the deer's hair. It tilted its tiny hat back on its head and began yelling at William in his squeaky voice.

"You should be in your home! Don't make us bite you little boy. You'll be so sick you won't be able to climb the tree to get back to your family!"

William cowered at the tick's voice.

"I don't want to get sick. I am looking for my friends, but no one seems to be around." William started, but the little tick interrupted him.

The tick laughed.

"That's because we are in charge of the forest now! No one is supposed to be out, and if they didn't listen, we bit them until they were sick! Now, get back to whatever tree you fell out of before we put someone on your head to ride you!"

William ran away before the tick could yell at him anymore. He ran until he was exhausted and plopped down on a rock to catch his breath. A field mouse was scurrying by and William waved. "Excuse me, sir," William gasped. "Where has everyone been?"

The field mouse paused, frowning. "I don't have time to talk. I have to get home to my sick children. They came out to play and the ticks bit them and chased them home. Everyone is home sick, and I suggest you go home before the ticks get you, too!"

The mouse hurried away, leaving William to sit and think about what the ticks had done. William became angry at the ticks for making everyone afraid to come out and for making his friends sick. The forest animals loved to come out and to see each other after winter had ended. The only person people were usually afraid of was the old mountain lion in the cave.

"Maybe if I go see him, he will tell me how to chase the ticks away," he thought. William gulped, and then set off to the old mountain lion's cave.

Despite his anger at the ticks, the little opossum cringed as he knocked on Gregg the mountain lion's door. He knocked a few times but no one came to answer.

Just as he was getting ready to leave, a shadow appeared behind him. "Can I help you, young man?" a gruff voice spoke. William turned to see Gregg the mountain lion staring down at him. He loomed over the little opossum, and William stared at his big teeth and long claws. He let out a low growl. "Don't worry, I'm not going to eat you. Besides, you're very small and would hardly fill me up."

He pushed past William and opened the door to his cave, motioning over his shoulder to follow him inside. He sat down and peered at the little opossum huddling in his doorway. "Why are you knocking on my door?" he asked.

"P-please sir," William stammered. "My name is William. The ticks are bullying all of my friends in the forest. They made everyone sick, and are riding around on the deer, telling everyone what to do and where they are allowed to be! I need your help, because everyone is afraid of the ticks. They used to only be afraid -"

"Of me," the big cat interrupted, stroking his whiskers. He was quiet for a moment, and then spoke again. "I don't like bullies, and I especially don't like ticks. Who do they think they are, strutting around like they are in charge of the forest? And your friends are sick, you say?"

Gregg pondered for a second. "Before we go take care of these ticks, we must go see Sha, the old opossum at the top of the mountain. He will know how to make everyone better."

William fell in beside Gregg as they started up the mountain. As they made their way through the trees, William asked, "Why is everyone scared of you? Who is the opossum on top of the mountain?"

Gregg gave a growling chuckle.

"People are always scared of things that they don't understand, and they are scared of me because they haven't gotten to know me. I like to pretend I'm big and mean, and people leave me to do the things I need to do to take care of the forest. In times of need like this, it's up to people like us to take care of the people around us. We see something wrong and from a mountain lion like me down to a tiny opossum like you, we are responsible for caring for the ones around us. Now, the old opossum, Sha, is a good friend. He studies nature and finds the herbs we need to help people feel better. As you know it's very hard for opossums to get sick and so he tries to find ways to make everyone as healthy as you! One day he went to the top of the mountain to make his potions and he never came back down.

At the top of the mountain there was an enormous tree and William could see a opossum house nestled into its branches. "Hello!" Gregg bellowed, and William jumped at the roar. "Hello Sha, old friend. Come say hello to a tired old cat and a young opossum who needs our help!"

Sha came out of the house, leaning on his cane. "Why Gregg I thought that was you. And who is this, a opossum who needs help? My, my he is a little thing. What can I do to help the two of you?"

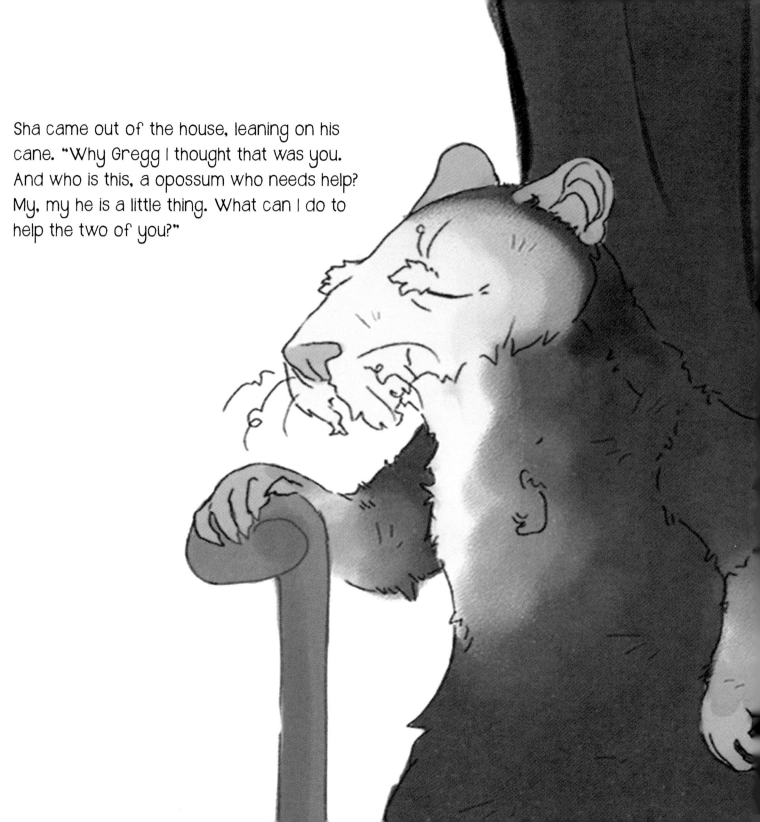

"Sir," William started, "Gregg said you have potions, he said maybe you could help my friends get better." Gregg rested a paw on William's shoulder as he joined the conversation.

"The ticks are up to their old tricks again." The forest animals are sick and the ticks are riding around telling everyone what to do."

Sha shook his head. "Those ticks are always up to no good. I came up this mountain a long time ago to work on this potion just for dealing with those horrible little pests. Well I know just the thing to help everyone get better and I think I know how we can chase those horrible ticks out of the forest. Let me get my bag and we will go back to the opossum village in the forest and see about getting things back to normal."

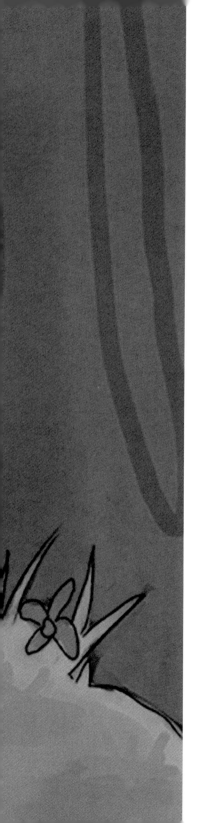

William grinned a toothy grin. "I know my family will be thrilled to help, but they won't be happy to hear that everyone is sick! Can we ask them to help us, too?" The old opossum grinned back. "That is precisely what we need, my boy! We will need all the opossums in the forest to help!" With that the old opossum disappeared into his house to find his bag.

The trio started back down the mountain, with Gregg and Sha excitedly catching up on how each other had been for the past few years. After a short time, William, who had been lost in thought, piped up. "Excuse me, Sha. Why do we opossums not get sick? I know that sometimes we can wake up and the ticks will be there, biting us. Why are we not sick like everyone else?"

"Well, William, we are a strong animal in the forest, and we are fairly healthy. We don't get colds and we rarely get sick. This is because we are made differently; so while everyone else might get sick, it is our job to be ready to help them get better. That's why I live on top of the mountain and try to learn how to make new potions every day."

Gregg spoke up.

"Now that we are back in the forest, you two go round up the rest of the opossums. I will start searching the forest for the ticks and I'll chase them towards the opossum neighborhood. Once I have them corralled, you can all save the deer and get the ticks once and for all."

A short time later a roar echoed through the trees, making everyone's teeth rattle and the youngest animals shake with fear. A stampede of hooves rang out as Gregg began herding all the deer. The ticks riding them screamed in fear, pulling the deer and trying to steer them away. No matter what they did though, the deer kept running, for even they were nothing compared to Gregg.

As the deer ran frantically through the trees, shying away from Gregg's fierce teeth, Meg and the rest of the opossum began to attack. Uncurling on their long tails, they hung down from the trees and snatched the ticks from the deer's heads. The ticks were so distracted by the deer that they never knew what chomped them until it was too late.

Finally Meg called out to the opossum family. "We've won! The ticks are gone, we've won!"

The animals scooped up William from his tree branch and Gregg too, despite his growl. "Hooray for William! Hooray for Gregg! You've helped the forest and saved the day!"

A cheer went up through the forest. William clambered down from the home tree to meet Sha and a heavy breathing Gregg. As he came to the bottom of the tree the forest animals started to come out from their homes. Some were excited and cheering, but others had the same tired and sad expression that the deer wore.

"William!" Sha said with excitement as he unslung his bag. "Quick, my boy, I need you to help me give everyone my potion!" With that he began pulling small bottles out and handing them to William. William started to scamp away, but Meg caught up with him.

"Here," she said, helping him carry the bottles. "Let me help you! We'll go find all our sick friends."

Before long, the forest animals were starting to feel like their old selves again. As the sun started to set and the animals began to celebrate, a tired Gregg turned away from the happy animals to return to his cave. William smiled and waved goodbye to his big friend; the mountain lion shrugged, but smiled to himself as he disappeared into the dusk.

Approximately 25% of all patients that get Lyme disease are children between the ages of 5-14. In some states like Pennsylvania, 85% of all ticks carry some communicable infection including Lyme disease. Protecting our children by focusing on prevention is vitally important. Parents must include the following steps into their going outdoors routine:

• Avoid areas where ticks hang out. This includes tall grass, wooded areas, leaf piles, and brush. Stay on trails when hiking.
• Liberally apply tick repellent when outdoors. Especially from the waist down.
•Wear light-colored clothing – Makes it easier to spot ticks.
•Have your child wear a hat when in the woods.
•Wear long pants and long sleeves, if possible, and tuck pants into socks.
• Immediately throw clothing in hot dryer for 15 minutes to kill ticks. If clothes are wet throw in dryer for an hour. Ticks will survive a wash cycle.
• Do tick checks when returning from the outdoors. Check the entire body but carefully examine dark, moist areas like behind the knees, groin, armpits, and back of neck.
• When bathing, remember an attached tick will not wash off from a shower but can be dislodged if not attached.
• Check your outdoor pets for ticks which reduces the chances of a tick being carried indoors and transferred to a child.

These steps take time but are worth every second when it comes to protecting a child from a potential lifetime of chronic illness.

-Bob Miller, CTN
Tree of Life Health

57668592R00024

Made in the USA
Columbia, SC
11 May 2019